MW01229068

A

SINNERS

REDEMPTION

Searching For My Soul

By Kandy Kaine

A SINNERS REDEMPTION: SEARCHING FOR
MY SOUL

Copyright © 2019 KANDY KAINE

Copyright © 2019 LIBRARY OF CONGRESS.

US Copyright.gov

All right reserved

Printed in the United States of America.

All rights reserved.

This book is a work of fiction. Names, characters, places, and incidents either are the product of the author's imagination or are used fictitiously and are not to be construed as real. Any resemblance to actual persons, living or dead, business establishments, events, or locales, is entirely coincidental.

No part of this book may be used or reproduced in any manner whatsoever without prior written consent of the publisher and author, except in the case of brief quotations embodied in critical articles and reviews.

Dedications:

I dedicate this book to every person out there who had to endure the pain and struggles of being a Christian. To those who were told that you were only to live a certain way just to fit in. This book if for all the ministers, pastors, preachers, and teachers who forgot that they were once children too. To all the young people who are trying to figure out if they will go to Heaven or Hell because of a choice that they made based off of someone telling them to. This book if for all the people that were turned away from churches because of the way that they dressed, looked, or lived their lives. God said come as you are. We have no place to judge anyone for the lack there of, nor how they are born. We are supposed to uplift and love one another. This is for all the teenagers who are scared to face their loved ones and tell them how they feel when following your dreams and what's in your heart. Do not be forced into a way of living that is not suitable for you. As long as you have God in your mind, heart and soul; you can never go wrong with him….

Acknowledgements:

First and foremost, I want to give honor to God. He is the head of my life and my household. Any book that I write I am guided by him with faith. Second, I want to say I love you to my boys. I'm still writing so that I can make sure they don't see me fail. Life is only what you make of it, so if you put your mind to it; you can do it. Next, my fiancé AJ. I want you to know that I am grateful and blessed to have such a wonderful, loving, understanding, willing, helpful, and most of all supportive girlfriend in the whole wide world. I love you, babe. Without you, a lot that I have to do will not be done. You have helped me with book sales, you have purchased every book that I have written. You have promoted me even when I wasn't promoting myself. The support that you give is beyond amazing. I just want to say thank-you. To my mother, without you, I wouldn't even be here. I'm grateful to have a supportive mother who is encouraging and loving. Picking up a gift that you have is a blessing. Without your words of encouragement and talent; I wouldn't have come this far. I want to say that you are my inspiration. It began with you; I love you, mom. This is still the beginning. I will not stop until I know that my calling is complete.

Shout Outs:

Kindall, Kamron, Amanda (my wife), My Mom, You four are my main inspiration. Without you I would have not come this far. I just want to make my mark and secure a future for us all. I am glad to have the support I have from the four of you if I don't get it from anybody else. I promise that all this hard work I'm doing will pay off in the end for us all. We are in this together. Thank you for being the reasons why I will continue writing until LMN calls me LOL. We are headed to making books into movies!! A few more Tiffany Gilbert, Chy Seoul, Mya Shay, Tiyell Barns, Lanie Frits, Tanisha Adams, Erika Lantanya, Desaree, Raven Bennett, C. Monet, Meysha Llyod, Destiny Sky, Quanna, Ebonee Abby, Keisha Starr, Myia White, and many more. Thanks to all of you for still rooting for me to be better at my craft, and telling me to never give up.

SYNOPSIS:

Growing up in an apostolic church your told the right ways and the wrong ways of being a Christian. You are only allowed to dress a certain way, speak a certain way, and live a life free from sin. But as a sinner you live free as a bird. Armoni at a young age had to learn the hard way. With parents as pastors of the church; everything she did was critiqued. Sorting through her life trying to please her loved ones and friends, Armoni has decide which life she wants to live. Singing in the church choir trying to follow in her sisters footsteps; to only be told she wasn't good enough. When Armoni gets a taste of the worldly life, she begins to rethink the whole Christian life; backsliding as they would call it. Armoni falls in love with the real world, but her family made it hard for her to be happy. Church became a nightmare when she had to choose between God and her worldly ways. Trying to please her friends and family; Armoni not only lost sight in herself but in her calling. When her gospel career is put on the line; Armoni has to choose between the two worlds. Will she please those near and dear to her, or follow her own dreams? Making the best choice for herself.

Prelude:

My name is Armoni Carmichael and I am the youngest of five children. We live in one of the busiest states in the whole world; Atlanta, GA. We moved here when my dad had to transfer for his job. I hated the fact that I was the youngest. My sister Leah was the oldest; she's 19. She is just so perfect. My mom and dad feel like she can do no wrong. But the things that I have seen her do; baby listen. She wouldn't be alive. Even though I'm only 12; I wish my parents would just let up.

Then I have twin brothers Drew and Donate' age 17. They are the football jocks in the family. They both play for King high school. They are always gone to football games or out with their friends, so I rarely see them. And lastly there is my sister Candise. She is 15 and she is always in her books. We go to the same school for now. She's the only one that I talk to. I guess since we are the youngest ones, we have more in common. Mom said that she was a genius, but I beg to differ. She was always doing something stupid that made me laugh. Anyone who talks in their sleep is no genius. Then there was me 4 foot 9 with long black hair and a pretty smile, and I am in the 6th grade.

My parents have been married for over twenty years. Leanne and Donald Carmichael. They met when they were in high school, and I guess fell in love. Born and raised in California; they left once they had my oldest sister. At that time, they wasn't married, and I guess my mom parents kicked her out. I guess back then it was normal for kids to just up and leave. They moved to Atlanta because of my dad's job and never looked back. They both went to college and graduated, and then started having more kids. After they had me I guess they felt like they had enough.

Being the youngest child had its ups and downs. I got whatever I wanted, but I also got a lot of hand-me-downs. They were still good clothes and shoes though. My parents never bought anything that was cheap, nor was it in bad shape. I always had my hair done, and I always had my nails groomed. We were told that we had to look nice because we were reflections of our parents.

At 12 years old I already knew what I wanted to be when I grew up, but as always my parents felt like they had the final say so. I want to become a singer. My favorite singers are Yolonda Adams, Aaliyah, and Whitney Houston. I found myself singing in the mirror every morning, or any chance I could get. I did talent shows at church since I was three, it was what I loved.

I sing in the children's choir, but I wanted to sing in the adult choir. They always go to sing the better songs. The kids choir only got to sing for the holidays or on H.Y.P.U nights. My older sister and my mom was in the choir too, and they were the ones who always got to sing. It made me mad as h-e double hokey stick. I wasn't allowed to say the real word because it was a sin.

Speaking of sins, well we all had some. My parents tell me every day that I needed to repent. If I had got an attitude with my her she would throw holy oil on me and pray. We weren't able to do anything that was remotely close to a sin. My clothes were baggy, and my hair was always pulled up into a ponytail. I wasn't allowed to ware any tight closes, makeup, nor nail polish; well the polish had to be a nude or clear color.

They are the kind of parents that you see in the movies. They never fight, argue, nor curse. I swear I feel like they are robots. My dad is the pastor of his own church too. My mom says that we have to be rooted in the blood of Jesus in order to go to heaven; whatever that means. We go to church four days out of the week. Wednesday nights we had Evangelist service and or youth night. Thursday night was choir rehearsal; which I had to sing. Then on Fridays we had to go to bible study, and there was two services on Sunday. We lived in the church.

Today was going to be a long day. My mom and dad was making me get baptized. Some of the members made it their business to run their mouth about it. Said that I should have gotten baptized when I was a baby; being that my parents ran the church. It was none of their business anyway. One thing I learned about my mom and her church friends was that they gossiped a whole lot. They told everybody's business if they had something to tell.

Anyway, today was Saturday. On these days I would be hanging with my friends. They didn't like church, nor did their parents force them to go. I invited them, but I guaranteed that they won't show. Getting ready I had to put on this long skirt that went all the way to my ankles, and a shirt that was to my neck. I wouldn't say I was uncomfortable, but my mom could loosen up. The dress code they have is for old people.

It was 6:00pm and we were all ready to head to the church. My parents were dressed up in their matching colored church clothes, and my sisters and brother was ready as well. Me on the other hand, I was not at all ready. I was having second thought about being baptized just to sing in the adult choir in four years. Looking in the mirror at myself I knew that I was going this for one reason and one reason only. I WANTED TO SING!!

"Armoni are you ready?" my mom called out to me.

"Yes ma'am. Here I come. I was putting on my stockings."

"You have to hurry up. We have to be the first people there to unlock the doors," she replied with a calm voice.

"Yes ma'am."

I was beyond nervous, but I knew I had to get it out the way. Having people watch me and being dipped in that cold water scared me. I just wanted to sing, and if I had to get my hair soaked to do it I was down for it. We arrived at the church thirty mins until six. My palms were sweating, and my knees were shaking. A million and one things was running through my mind. There was only one thing that was going to calm me down. I put my head down and I prayed.

"Father God in the name of Jesus. I really need you right now. I really don't understand why I am so nervous about being baptized, but I am. I need you to let me know that I am doing your will. If this is what I have to do to sing for you lord; I'm willing. This is a major change in my life. Once I am baptized then I have to let go of my worldly friends and possessions. Lord my voice is a gift from you, and I promise to use it just for you. In the name of Jesus, I pray. AMEN......

When we walked into the church I felt a lot better. Everybody was coming in after us. They all began to take their seats close to the baptism pool. I headed to the front of the sanctuary. Everyone began to sing and that's when I knew it was time. My dad walked up to the podium with his robe on and his bible in his hand. He began to sing along with them and motioned for me to come stand next to him. As they continued to sing my dad began to speak.

"Heavenly father, I just want to thank you for letting us come together on this special day. You have called my youngest child to join us. She is willing to give her life to you on this day," he prayed.

When I looked at my mother she was behind us crying, and the whole church was praying. I know that I was supposed to have my head down praying, but it was a sight to see. Looking to see if any of my friends had showed up, I became disappointed. Not one of them was sitting in the pews. I became upset, but then my dad nudged me to put my head back down as he prayed.

After about ten minutes of them praying and singing I sat back down. The spirit began to move, and everybody started crying. I never really understood why they were shouting and speaking in a weird way. My dad always told me that they got the holy spirit. I still didn't understand. After thirty minutes it was time for me to be baptized. They started singing wait in the water as I got into the pool. The water was freezing cold, and I wasn't happy at all. My dad looked me in the eyes.

"Are you ready to except Jesus into your life?" he asked me.

"Yes sir," I replied. As soon as I said that he leaned me back in the freezing cold water. I was livid.

"Hallelujah!" he shouted. "Yes Lord. Guide my baby down the path of righteousness. Take over her vessel and cleanse her with your holy spirit."

The whole time he was talking I was thinking to myself, *"Can you get me out this cold pool now."* My father never knew when it was time to stop talking. Majority of the time my mother has to step in, and she did just that. She guided me out the pool placing towels over my soiled clothes. We went down stairs to the preachers bathroom, so I could change. When I was just about done; my mother walked up to me, grabbed my face, and kissed me on my forehead.

"What was that for mama?" I asked.

"Because I am proud of you. You have finally turned your life over to Jesus. This is the happiest day of my life," she explained. She had tears running down her face. Tears of joy; glad that I was following her footsteps. "All you have to do now is live right. No more sinning."

I didn't say another word. She hugged me as I hugged her back. I loved my mom, but I wasn't quite sure what she was meant. What was really considered a sin? And why was it so important for me not to do it? I was anxious to find out. This was just the beginning of my journey. I had a lot to learn about being Christian, and what a better way to learn by experiencing it myself.

Chapter 1: Lead Me Not Into Temptations

Sitting in my room I was not quite ready for school. I was debating on what I wanted to ware. Since I got baptized a few of years ago, I had to really be perfect. At first it bothered me not being able to ware what I wanted, or do what I wanted to do but it wasn't all that bad. I was a teenager now and I really wanted to come into my own look. I had breast, a big but and some curvy hips. Since I was a Christian I had to keep it all covered up.

My parents were really strict on me now that I was in high school. They had a lot more rules that I had to follow, and they were very uptight. I had never seen them this uptight with me with any of my other siblings. It was like since I was the baby, they had to be extra careful. My sisters got into a lot of trouble over the years, and one of my bother Drew was a dad now. He and his girlfriend ended up having a baby boy. My parents were upset with him, but he's an adult.

My oldest sister still lived at home too, but she was in college not that far away, and Candise and I went to the same school; for now. I was glad I at least had somebody at school with me. It got pretty boring at times when my friends wasn't around. I only had two of them, but they were just like me "Church Girls". There was one girl at my school I thought I was friends with, but she was a some-timer.

In the next two days it will be my 15th birthday, but I knew I wasn't going to have a party. My parents didn't do stuff like that. To them a birthday party was just us and dinner at the table. Nobody was able to come unless they went to church with us. I really didn't like the girls that I went to school with because they were jerks. They always felt like they were better than everyone. But this year I wanted a normal party like the kids at school had.

It took me about thirty minutes to get myself ready for school. My parents had already left for work, so I had to make my own breakfast. The outfit that I chose to ware was a long tan skirt with some black flats, and a short sleeve black shirt. It had a necklace attached to it. My friends at school laughed at me about it, but I didn't really care, I was some-what comfortable. After I got dressed I went down stairs to make me a bowl of captain crunch. It was my all-time favorite cereal. My brothers and sisters had already left. Being the youngest I got used to being left behind, or being left out.

Today was going to be a busy day. After school I had to rush to the church. Today was Thursday, so I had choir rehearsal. Even though I was quite 16 yet my parents let me sing anyway. I gathered my things for school off the dining room floor and headed out the door. As I began to walk down the street two guys from my school came behind me.

"You look stupid waring that in this hot weather," one of them yelled.

"You know she a church girl," the other one said to his friend. "Aye church girl! Is it true what they say; the preachers daughters are freaks?"

I just kept walking. It was bad enough that they were talking stuff, but I had to see them in school every day. I knew being a Christian came with a lot of issues, but I never knew it was this bad. I took my bible with me everywhere I went, and every time somebody always said something to me. At times it upset me and at times I just ignored it.

Once I made it to school I sat on the front steps and read a few verses out of my brand-new King James. The kids were all looking at me funny and snickering. If they only knew about Jesus then maybe just maybe they would understand how I felt. God was a major part of my life and I was happy about it.

When I went into the building I headed straight to the cafeteria. Since I had already eaten at home; I sat at one of the empty tables alone. I didn't mind that I was alone. I guess since I was saved or as they would see it being better than them, they turned their noses up at me. It bothered me a lot at first but then I got use to it. I was a really genuine person and it was there loss not wanting to be friends with me.

After breakfast I went to three classes before I had lunch. I went to English, Spanish class, and social studies. After lunch I had math, science, history and gym. Today wasn't as bad as other days. I guess since we had a lot of test to take nobody bothered me. Some of the guys would grab at my clothes, or just make fun of me. The girls would just laugh. All I did was say a prayer in my head hoping that they would leave me alone. I got out of school at 4pm, that was the best part of my day.

When I walked home I took a short cut to avoid all the other kids. I really didn't want to be bothered. I buried my head into my bible and just kept walking, but as soon as I got on my street I could tell it was going to be a problem. There were some kids standing in front of the corner store who would always bother everyone. With my head still in my bible I tried walking pass.

"Where are you going little mama?" one of the guys asked me. He pulled on my arm and I dropped my bible.

"I'm going home," I replied picking it up off the dirty ground.

"What is this crap your reading?" he asked, snatching my bible out of my hand. "Oh, you one of them Christian chicks ain't you?" he asked taunting me. He waved my book up in the air as his friends begin to laugh.

"Give me that back!" I yelled, trying to get it from his hands. "I'm not playing give it back.

"What are you going to give me if I give it back?"

"Nothing. Just give me back my bible." He looked at me with a weird grin on his face. I reached in for my bible once more then grabbed me. "Let me go!" I yelled.

"Na ma. That's not what I want. I want you to give me a kiss; church girl," he demanded.

"NO! NOW GIVE ME MY BIBLE!"

Before I knew it his lips met mine. He then began to stick his tongue down my throat. I was trying my best to push him off of me, but he was way too strong. I wasn't sure how to get out of his grasp. As I kept shoving him he dropped my bible on the ground and grabbed me even tighter. Once he let me go I picked up my bible and ran home. I just felt so dirty, and I knew that had my parents saw me I would have been in big trouble.

"You know you like it," the other guys taunted me."

"LET ME GO!" I yelled again, and he did. They all started to laugh.

I ran in the house passed everyone and went into the bathroom. Tears filled my eyes as I washed my mouth out with soap and water. Then suddenly something came over me. I became conflicted with feelings and emotions. That was my very first kiss. I begin to question why he kissed me. Nobody has ever did that to me; ever. I knew that if I had told my parents then I would have gotten into a lot of trouble. I went to bed with a lot of confusing things on my mind. I kind of wanted to see what is was like to have a boyfriend now. knowing how my parents would react I would have to keep it to myself.

Chapter 2: Happy Sweet 16

"Armoni! I need you to get up out of that bed sweetie," my mom yelled out to me.

"But mom I want to just lay here. It's way too early." I looked over at my clock and it was 7:00am. "Mom it's only seven in the morning."

"Armoni can you come down here please? I'm not going to ask you again."

"Armoni, do what your mother says and come down here!" my dad yelled out to me.

Sucking my teeth, I rolled out the bed. I threw on my robe and my slippers. Wiping the sleep from my eyes I headed down stairs to see what they wanted. When I made it to the bottom of the stairs I didn't see any one.

"Mom, Dad, where is everyone?" I called out. There was still no answer. I went into the kitchen, the living room, and the basement. I still didn't see them.

"Come on you guys stop playing," I said again. It was

weird. My parents had just called me to come down stairs. I

called out for my brothers and sisters; even they didn't

answer. That's when I noticed that the front door was open.

"What in the world is going on?" I asked myself. I opened

the screen door and still didn't see anyone. When I walked

down the stairs to see if my parents car was gone……

"SURPRISE!!!" They all yelled.

I placed my hands over my face to try and stop the

tears from coming down my face. I was beyond surprised.

My family was jumping up and down screaming. I was so

surprised that I didn't notice that they were standing in the

driveway in front of this brand-new Nissan Altima.

"Is this for me!" I asked with excitement.

"Yes baby, it's for you," my mom responded. She grabbed my arm and walked me to the driver door. As she grabbed my hand she placed in it a single key.

"NOOO WAY!"

"You deserve it sweetie," my dad added. I wasn't expecting this at all. My brothers and sisters were still cheering.

"Twins why didn't yawl tell me?" I asked them. They looked at each other and laughed. "Fa real, this can't be mine."

"I mean if you don't want it; I will take it," my sister Leah said.

"Girl right, I will take it sis if you don't want it," Candise added.

"I just wasn't expecting this." I got into my brand-new car checking out the interior. "This is nice."

"We are glad you like it. Now before you can drive it you have to get your license. Leah can teach you how to drive it every day after school," said my mother.

"Now I didn't agree to that," Leah said laughing.

After I looked at my brand-new car for a few more minutes it was time for me to go to school. My mind was racing, and my feelings were everywhere. I wanted to drive my car to school so that I could show it off. I also wanted to show that boy who kissed me that I had it. Then maybe he would see that I wasn't a little girl. I was 16 now and I was a woman.

I was ready to get my day over with. I knew no one at school would remember that today was my birthday, so I didn't care if I wasn't given anything. I got ready for school and headed on my way. I walked the same exact way as I always did every day. This time my sister Candise decided to walk with me. I guess since I was older she didn't look at me as a baby anymore. We walked in silence for a bit until I said something.

"Candi, have you ever kissed a boy before?" I asked her.

"Yeah, I was your age and mama caught me. She made me read from the bible every day after school."

"I thought she made you do that for bible study."

"Oh noo. See Willy a guy from church asked me to walk home with him after choir rehearsal. When we reached the house; he kissed me, and mom had pulled up. Her face was red as the devil himself."

"Was you scared?"

"No. Mom keeps forgetting that we are still young. They used to do the same things as kids as we do now. I fake it to make it just to make mom happy."

"So, your sinning?" I asked because I just wanted to be sure I wouldn't go to hell because of a kiss.

"Look sis; I believe in God don't get me wrong, but it's just some things that I know isn't true. You will find out sooner or later. Let me guess you had your first kiss?"

"Well not exactly. I was walking home from school the other day; well I don't know Candi he just kissed me."

"Do you know the boy Armoni?"

"Kind of. He lives on our street, and he's a street boy. I always thought he was cute, but since we are saved I didn't want to get in trouble," I explained.

"But you are human. You didn't say anything to mama did you?"

"No. I just kept it to myself. You know how mama is. Everything or anything we say or do is a sin. You remember when Leah got her tongue pierced; mama kicked her out the choir and made her sit for weeks. Then mama made her get baptized again."

"Yeah I thought that was a bit much. Well like I said sis your human."

I went into school thinking about everything Candi said. No matter what we do our parents called it a sin. If I wasn't mistaken our parents had Leah way before they were married, and I know they did other stuff. When I got to school it was like any other normal day. Nobody said a word to me. I went home after a long day, and irritation. I ended my Monday night reading my bible and going to bed. I wrote in my diary until I fell asleep.

Dear Diary:

Lord; I am conflicted right now with my feelings. I know that there is a lot of things that we are not allowed to do because we are Christians, but it's hard. Mom says that if we do right by you then we will get into heaven, and I am ok with that. I just don't understand how come we get

punished for small things like kissing. What could really go

wrong from kissing. I can see if it was something bad like

killing someone or stealing. I know as a Christian we are

supposed to live right just like you did, but I am new to this

kind of life. I only know what my parents show and tell me,

but I don't understand the bible. I just want to live my life

right and be happy doing it. Well it's about time for me to

go to bed. I hope you understand how I feel; I just want to

be happy.

Chapter 3: H. Y. P. U Service

Since my birthday I was conflicted about my feelings. My parents ended up throwing me a party, but it was at the church. I knew that they wasn't going to let me have any of my friends over. My sisters thought it was funny that I was in church celebrating my 16th birthday. Talk about being really embarrassed. My parents being pastors were the worst. It was so many things that I wanted to do, but to them it's not "Godly" like.

Today was Saturday, and I had some plans. I wanted to go to a skating party that they were having at our local skate rink, but asking my parents was the hard part. When I got out the bed, I brushed my teeth, and washed my face. I had my own bathroom in my room, so I didn't get interrupted no matter how long I took. I stared at myself in the mirror. Being sixteen I noticed that my breast were way bigger than they were before, and my hips and butt was spreading. Underneath my church clothes I had no clue that I was filling up. I couldn't stop admiring myself.

Getting ready for today I had to pick out my outfit before I went down stairs. Looking in my closet; I couldn't find anything worth waring to the party. As I was still looking; my sister Leah barged in my room.

"What are you doing little sis?" she asked, as she plopped her body on my bed.

"Nothing, looking for an outfit for tonight."

"Oh, for H.Y.P.U night?"

"Um….. No," I said looking at her with a confused face. "I'm not going to that. I was going to the skating rink tonight. They have a party going on. I wasn't told anything about a church function." I stepped out my closet and put a skirt up to my body. I wasn't trying to hear nothing about church. "Mama said we had to go?"

"Um yeah. You know we all have to go, and you know we all have to lead worship too."

I threw the skirt down on the bed that I was still holding. I was getting really fed up with all this church stuff. We can never have any fun that kids should have. I sat on the bed next to my sister and I fell back.

"Leah have you ever been kissed before?" I asked her hoping she wouldn't get upset.

"Um… Yeah a few times. Why? You have a boyfriend or something?"

"No. Well a boy from school kissed be a couple of weeks ago."

"Was that it?" she asked smiling at me.

"Yeah, that was it. I mean you know how mom and dad is. *"Kissing is a sin, Having sex before marriage is a sin, this is a sin, that is a sin."* I can't see how you do it. your almost 23. I would have been left."

"Well since I'm in college here in Atlanta; I just stay here until I can get my own place. Plus, its better here than on campus. Trust me, what mom doesn't know won't hurt her."

"Yeah I guess. So how will I get out of church tonight? I really want to go to this party."

"I have no clue. That's something your going to have to figure out yourself, little sis," she said, after tapping me on the head.

I was confused with feelings at this point. Since it was still early I had all day to come up with a plan. I had finally made my way down stairs where everyone else was. My brothers were already gone to football practice and Candi had left for work. My parents were sitting on the couch preparing for tonight's service, and Leah was in the kitchen. I sat in the reclining chair and sighed.

"What's wrong my angel?" my mom asked me.

"Nothing. What's Leah cooking?"

"Your fathers favorite... Omelets."

"Oh... So, we have to do H.Y.P.U service tonight?" I asked with a shy voice.

"Yes, and you're the M.C. You know that since you joined the choir you have to lead the service tonight. Why? Did you have something else in mind?"

"Well..." As I was about to say something Leah came into the living room with dads plate.

"So Armoni, did you ask mom about the skating party?" she said winking at me.

"What skating party?" my dad asked.

"It's a party the skating rink has every year. I was going to ask if I could go for just a bit. I really want to go. So...... Can I? Please?"

"I think not," my dad responded. "You think your going to pass up church just to go skating? Not going to happen. Now go get dressed we have some errands to run."

I looked at my mom to see if she was going to say something, but she didn't. She just sat there. Leah tapped me on the top of my head.

"Sorry little sis, I tried." I got up from the chair and followed behind her.

"I don't want to go to church tonight. What can I do to get out of it?" I asked going into the kitchen.

"Maybe you can fake sick, or tell him you have a report to do for school. What ever you decide; make sure you don't get caught."

I took what she said into consideration. I was stuck trying to figure out what I was going to do. I never lied to my parents before, and I never missed church before. I was 16 and I wanted to have some fun. I didn't know that being a Christian was this hard. I could only imagine how he would feel if I was a lesbian. That would have been all bad. My father call lesbians an abomination and a sin that needed to be taken off the earth. I don't agree with him because God loves everyone. My parents are as holy as they come. Christians that automatically get into heaven for being a pastor and a pastors wife.

Three Hours Later

It was about that time for us to leave for church. I was dragging myself to get dressed. My parents were already down stairs with my brothers and Candi waiting on me. Leah somehow found a way to get out of going, so I began to think of what I could say to not go either.

"Armoni lets go honey!" my mom yelled.

"I'm not ready yet," I responded back.

"Come on sis, I need to practice before service," Candi stated.

"Hold on. I'll be right down."

Still not sure how I was going to get out of going tonight, I just got dressed and went anyway. I wasn't like Leah; bold and able to stand up for herself. I was way too afraid of my parents, and I didn't feel like hearing my dad preach to me over and over.

As we all got into the car my dad turned on his gospel cd that he played every day. He had a mixture of artist that he listened to. His favorite artist was Hezekiah Walker. I can't even lie I sing every single time when gospel music comes on. It was like I was on stage singing it with them.

The church was about twenty minutes away from the house, but it was only five minutes away from the skating rink. When we drove passed it I seen all the kids walking in. I looked down at my watch and it was 6:30. I still had time to go if I could. Plopping back in my seat; sucked my teeth and wished my parents would have change their minds.

"Are you ready to lead service Armoni?" my mom asked, turning around in her seat.

"Yeah I guess," I replied, with an attitude.

"Yeah?" my dad said correcting me.

"Yes ma'am."

"You're going to do great. Leah does an amazing job when she leads the youth service."

"Well I'm not Leah," I replied. I got annoyed. I didn't even want to sing anymore. They always compared me to her.

We pulled up to the church and everyone else followed behind us. Cars loaded with children was walking into the church. As I got out the car my parents were already at the door greeting the members. My twin brothers and Candi were inside setting up. Closing the car door behind me; I ran into one of the Deacons sons.

"Excuse you!" I yelled at him.

"I'm sorry sister Armoni," he apologized. "You look very beautiful tonight," he added.

"Thanks," I replied holding my head down. "Your Deacon James son right?"

"Yeah. Are you singing tonight? You have a very anointed voice," he said.

I pulled my hair back behind my ear and walked into the sanctuary. None of the younger guys in the church have ever spoken to me. I always thought I was way too ugly for them to even say hi. I made my way up to the microphone and when I looked up he was staring at me. My throat became clogged as the music from the piano and guitar began to play.

"Praise the Lord everybody," Amy said. She was another youth super singer. "Tonight, is H.Y.P.U night. So, you know that means your in the hands of the young people. While everyone is coming in Armoni will start us off with a song." I looked at her then I looked back at Preston. He was still staring.

"Praise the Lord everyone."

"Praise the Lord!" they yelled back." I cleared my throat and opened my mouth.

"Come on come on come on, don't you wanna go? Come on come on come on, don't you wanna go? Come on come on come on, don't you wanna go? Don't you wanna ride that train?" I sang. Everyone began to sing along with me. The nerves in my body started to take over me as my parents took their seats. I then changed the song. "What a mighty God we serve. What a mighty God we serve.

Angels bow before him. Heaven and earth adore him. What

a mighty God we serve."

My mom was smiling from ear to ear watching me

sing and not mess up. Even though I wanted to go skating; I

was enjoying my time at church. We sang a few more

songs until it was time to read the scripture. Some of the

other youth members did the welcome address and did the

offering.

After being up there for about fifteen minutes it was

time for us to take our places in the choir stand. I just knew

that my dad was going to make me sing. But instead he let

someone else do it. I stood their upset and mad. The one-

time Leah doesn't sing he lets someone else do it. I swayed

back and forth mouthing the words. We sung four songs

then my dad let the oldest of the youth do the sermon.

When Justin got up on the podium I couldn't help but notice that he kept pulling at his pants. It was funny and weird. Every time he would fix them he would walk away from the podium. He looked at me and winked at me.

"Sister Armoni did a wonderful job starting off tonight's service; Amen," he said.

He was the second guy to even say anything to me today or about me. I began to blush. I looked at my dad and he made a angry face. I knew that meant to stop smiling. I put my head back down.

"Amen," everyone else replied.

"Now tonight I'm going to talk about giving your soul to the Lord. Now we have some young folks in here that are scared to do that, but I'm here to say that it's ok. You cant be scared to want to be closer to Jesus; Amen."

"Amen," I said really loud.

"Amen," he said looking back at me.

"Now as the youth of this church we have to live right, walk right , and talk right. We cant be half stepping; Amen."

Everybody was agreeing with him. He went on and on about how the young people of the church was going to be the future of the church. Said that we all had to make sure we did everything as a kid to be right as adults. In the back of my mind I was wondering what was going on at the skating party. He kept talking and I kept blocking him out. I know we had to live right, but why couldn't we have any fun. We were still children.

He went on to talk for another twenty minutes then he ended. My dad went back to the podium and he told everyone to meet him down stairs for evening dinner. The whole time that service was going on my mom was down stairs cooking. I wasn't hungry; I was just ready to go home. I watched everyone eat and stayed to myself. That's when Justin sat next to me.

"So, your just going to sit here all alone sister Armoni?"

"Yeah, I'm not really hungry."

"You want to go with me to take these papers to my dads office?" he asked.

"Sure." We headed to his dads office alone, and he just kept talking to me.

"So, do you love singing?" he asked. It seemed like a stupid question to me.

"Yeah, I want to become a singer someday," I told him.

"I think you would be a great gospel singer."

"You think so?" I asked. It was like he was stroking my ego. Nobody really cared about how I felt.

"Yeah, I know so," he said as he placed his hand on my shoulder. "I've always enjoyed your singing." We walked into his dads office and he shut the door behind us.

"My sister Leah is the better sing……"

Before I could finish my sentence he kissed me. With tongue and all. Everything was running through my mind. What if we got caught? Stuck in the motion I kissed him back. This was my second kiss and I just wanted to see how it felt to kiss someone back. We stopped after a few minutes had passed. He looked at me and I looked at him; we both smiled. I walked out of his dads office glowing. His dad was a minister too. When I got back down stairs it was time for us to leave.

"Where did you go dear?" my mother asked.

"Oh, I was in the bible study room practicing a song for Sunday service," I lied.

"Oh, ok. That's wonderful, I cant wait to hear it."

Even though I didn't get to go to the skating party, my day ended perfect. I had the biggest smile on my face, and I finally felt liked, and important. Couldn't nobody tell me anything. I was 16; what harm could one little kiss do? When I got in the house I went straight to my room. I felt like I was floating on a cloud. I said not one word for the rest of the night.

Chapter 4: Being A Teenager

It had been about a month since the H.Y.P.U service and I still had that kiss on my mind. As a matter of fact, Justin and I had been talking a lot lately too. I guess since he was apart of the church my parents really didn't care. He was able to come over to see me as much as he wanted. I guess being a Ministers son had its perks.

Ever since my sixteenth birthday I had been begging my parents to let me drive the car that they had bought me, but they wouldn't. Now that Justin was in the picture; they said it was only ok if he was with me. Jason was 5"11 and he had his hair cut really short. He was light-skinned, so his hair was smooth as silk. His teeth were pearly white, and he was 17. He wasn't like any of the other guys I went to school with. He dressed to impress every day, so being with him was a plus.

As I was getting ready for school, my parents called me to come down stairs. I wasn't sure what was going on, but they sure sound like they were in a great mood.

"Armoni! Come on down here girl. You're going to be late for school," my mom repeated.

"Yes ma'am. Here I come," I replied back.

As I made it to the bottom steps with my bag draped over my shoulder; Justin was standing right in the dining room looking back at me. I just about stumbled over my two left feet. I had no idea that he was even coming nor walking me to school. Waving at him, he stood up and gave me a hug.

"Well don't you look pretty this fine Monday morning sister Armoni," he stated.

"You can just call me Armoni. And thanks, you look mighty handsome yourself. What are you doing here?" I asked in confusion.

"Don't be rude Armoni. He came to walk you to school. And afterwards he's going to take you driving," she said whispering in a funny voice.

"Oh really?" I asked smiling. "I thought Leah was going to help me. Did she not come home from school?"

"She started a new job."

"I don't mind teaching you. Plus, I'm not walking you, I'm driving you to school. I have my own car," he stated.

I looked up at him and smiled. I then looked at my parents as they smiled. What was so different about him taking me to school than a normal guy? I was cool with it. I guess they were letting up, but he was still a church boy. So, I knew he was going to be uptight. I gathered my things and we walked onto the porch.

"Thanks for doing this," I said. You really didn't have to you know."

"Yeah, I know. I came over to apologize to you about the kiss, and your parents asked me."

"Oh, they did? I'm sorry about that. Besides I kissed you back. So, there was no need to say sorry."

The sun was beaming, and the wind was blowing. The fresh air was gliding through my hair making it fly everywhere. Today I had decided to ware It down. I don't know why, but it just made me feel prettier. Jason opened his passenger door for me, and I waved goodbye to my parents. It was about time that they let me be a teenager.

As we began to drive down the street he turned on his radio to the gospel station. I was trying my hardest not to smile so hard, but I was really happy. He began to sing along with the music and so did I.

"So, what made you want to become a singer?" he asked, as he turned down the music.

"Well, I been singing ever since I can remember. My mom and sisters all sing, so I guess it was meant to be."

"But you can really sing though. Like really sing."

"I'm not all that. Am I?" I asked, being unsure of myself.

"Yeah," he replied, then placing his hand on mine. I blushed even harder. "Would you like to get something to eat before I drop you off?" he asked.

"Sure."

We drove around for about twenty minutes before we made it to the plaza. My mom had texted me to see if I had made it to school, but I ignored her. I knew she would have flipped out had she known we made a detour. I was enjoying myself for the very first time. What kind of harm could this cause. We are just to church friends getting something to eat before school. Besides he was the minister

Smith son, and he definitely wasn't going to go any further than kissing.

We pulled up to waffle house that was not that far from my school. Some of the seniors would come here on their lunch to eat, or skip school. This would be the first date that I ever had, and with a cute guy. I had to make sure I kept this a secret. I'm not sure if my parents would have agreed to all this.

"Is this place ok?" he asked parking the car.

"Yes, it's fine. I love their waffles," I replied.

"Me too. Were going to eat, then take you to school, I hope that's ok."

"Yeah, I don't like the schools breakfast anyway."

He smiled at me and got out the car. He then walked to my side and opened up my door. I was in such shock. he was being a gentleman. One thing my dad taught my brothers were to always be a gentleman. It was too cute.

His pearly white teeth smiling at me as he opened the restaurant door for me too.

"You are such a sweetheart," I said grinning.

"I try. You want to sit in the front at a table or a booth?" he asked me.

"I don't care. Where ever you want to sit."

I followed him to the both towards the window that was facing where my school was. Looking out I seen all the kids in my class go in, and others playing around. I didn't want them to see me with Justin, but then again if they did then maybe they would leave me alone. My mom called me again, so I answered it.

"Hello," I answered.

"Did you make it to school ok?" she asked.

"Yes ma'am. I'm actually right in front of it now," I lied.

"Did Justin be nice?" she scolded me. "He didn't do anything sinful did he?"

"No ma'am. He was such a gentleman."

"Good. Call me when you get out of school. I wont be home when you come and get the car. Please make sure you wear your seatbelt."

"Ok mom, I have to go. The school bells is ringing."

"Ok baby, I love you."

"I love you too mom." As soon as I hung the waitress greeted us.

"Welcome to Waffle House, my name is Jessica. Can I start you off with some coffee, or some orange juice?" she asked smiling at Justin.

"I'll have some water, and she can get what ever she wants," he said looking at me.

"And for you ma'am."

"I'll have some orange juice," I replied. I still wasn't sure what I wanted, but to be honest I wasn't all that hungry either.

"Are you guys ready to order? Or do you need more time?" she asked.

"I was going to have your grand slam just the way it comes."

"I'll just have a waffle, grits, eggs with cheese, and bacon."

"Is that all?" she asked again.

"Yes, that will be all," Justin added.

As she walked away I continued to watch the kids from my school get of the busses and walk in. Justin was playing with his watch not saying a word. I didn't say much either. We waited about eight minutes before our food had arrived. It was still quiet. We thanked our waitress for our food and she walked away.

"Thanks for bringing me to school. What time did you want to meet up later to go driving?"

"Well I don't get out of school until 4:00, but your mom said to come around 5:00. Said she wanted to make sure she was there when we left. Is she always that protective?"

"Yeah, she doesn't let me do anything. She says as Christians we had to live by the bible."

"Yeah, that's how my parents are. I know us being here is a big issue, I was hungry, and I wanted to treat you to breakfast. A pretty girl like you deserves to be treated right," he said touching my hand.

"Yeah, my dad would have a cow if he know I was here with you. But I am enjoying myself. You did a really good job on H.Y.P.U night."

"Awe thanks. I enjoyed your singing as well, I think you sing way better when your not shy," he said laughing.

I looked down at my watch and noticed that it was time for me to head into school. If I didn't hurry I wouldn't beat the late bell. I have never been late, but the way I was feeling I didn't mind. I was sitting across from a really cute guy. I was a junior in high school now, and I had to make sure I didn't screw up.

"I have to go Justin. The bell is about to ring. I don't want to be late,' I said wiping my face with a napkin.

"Ok, I'll pay for this," he said. "I'll meet you outside."

"Ok." I walked out the door and waited for him to pay for our bill. When he came out he had this crazy look on his face. "What's wrong?" I asked him.

"That girl just hit on me," he said laughing. "I told her I only had my eyes on one girl."

"Oh really," I said with my head down walking to the crosswalk. He did a slow run to catch up with me and grabbed my arm.

"I only have eyes for you Armoni," he said.

He then kissed me again. I couldn't help but to kiss him back. He wrapped his arms around me and held me close. It wasn't like the kiss that he gave me in church; it was way more sensual. I enjoyed every bit of it; nothing about it felt wrong. Once we stopped I heard the principal yelling for everyone to come in.

"I have to go Justin. I don't want to be late for school."

"Do you really have to go? I would love to hang with you."

"I cant Justin. My parents will kill me if they found out I skipped school. Look I will see you after school; I have to go," I said hugging him then running across the street.

I left him staring at me as I ran into the building. Apart of me wanted to stay with him, but I knew that it wasn't right. Plus, I was going to meet him after school. Being a junior in high school or a senior was very serious. I didn't want to miss anything that would hinder my grades. I just hope Justin understood that.

I went all day with Justin on my mind. It was kind of hard for me to really focus. He made me feel a way that I have never felt before. If my mama found out about our kiss she would have a cow, but I didn't care. I know being a Christian had rules, but what could one little kiss hurt? When school let out I went straight home. Sitting on the porch with my bible in my hands; I waited for my mom to come home. When 5:00pm hit she was pulling up. I was excited to start my driving lessons. She waved at me as she pulled into the driveway.

"Hey honey. Are you ready for your lessons?" she asked getting out the car.

"Yes ma'am. Justin isn't here yet though. He said he was going to be here when I got out of school."

"Well just give him some time honey. He is a senior in high school, and he has a lot of things to do at a junior minister at the church. Just give him some time," she said rubbing my cheek.

"Is your dad home yet?" she asked as she walked up the stairs.

"No ma'am, not yet. He must still be at work."

I waited and waited for Justin to show up, but he didn't. I never got his phone number to call him either to see where he was at. My dad didn't show up either. Around seven I went in the house to get my homework finished, eat and take my shower. Maybe something came up I thought to myself. I was sure why he stood me up after today, and I really didn't want to think about it anymore. It wasn't like we were dating anyway. Maybe his dad had him doing something for the church. My dad ended up coming in around 9pm and my mom had a mouthful for him. As I listened to them argue; knew that my mom was pretty upset. For the past couple of nights my dad had been coming in really late. I just pray that he wasn't cheating on my mom. He always told us to live by the word of God and never sin. He out of all people should know what to do and not to do. They argued all night until I dozed off. This was the first time my dad had ever came home late, and my mom wasn't happy about it.

Chapter 5: Sins and Secrets

Sitting in my room singing to myself I began to think about the date I had with Justin. It had been a few days since I had seen him. He made it seem as if he liked me, and I liked him too, but he still hadn't showed up. I wasn't sure what happened nor did my mom say anything about him coming. I just figured he was either busy or changed his mind. I went to choir rehearsal yesterday and two of the girls that I didn't really care for was talking about him. Since I was in the house of the Lord I didn't say anything. I would get my chance to speak with him on Sunday. I figured that he wouldn't even come to bible study tonight, so I wasn't really worried.

Getting ready for school, it was Friday which is test day. My parents was still here, but they weren't really speaking. My mom was really upset at my father. Maybe she knew something that we didn't. They always put on a front when they got around us and their friends, but I knew the truth. My mom was still mad at my dad for coming home late the other night. He said that he was at the church working, but she don't believe him. I was starting to think that he was hiding something, but as a Pastor why sin?

Dreading to go down stairs, waiting to hear the door slam but it didn't. the tension between them was so tight that you could cut it with a knife. So, I just snuck down anyway. I was trying my best to avoid them, or not make myself visible, but that didn't work. My mom caught me as soon as I reached the kitchen door.

"Hey Armoni, how's school going?" she asked.

"It's going ok mom. I have been looking at a few colleges to go to. I really want to go away for school."

"Don't you think that's a bad idea. I think it's a lot of temptations out in the world. You would be better off staying close to home. With you being saved and all."

"What does me being saved have to do with me wanting to go away for school mom? I think I can take care of myself. I don't want to be like Leah."

"I just don't think you should leave sweetie. Have you told your dad about this? I just don't want you to end up pregnant or on drugs. The church and being home is way better."

"Mom, you're not listening. I don't want to stay here for school. I really want to leave and follow my dreams as a singer."

"A singer. Your voice is not that good sweetie. You are not as good as your sister Leah. Keep singing in the choir and maybe your voice will get better. I'm just trying to protect you."

"Me leaving will not stop me from being a Christian. I know right from wrong mom. You and daddy had Leah before marriage. I know what to do and not to do," I said with an attitude.

"That was different Armoni. We were young and it was not how we planned it. I just want you to do things the way God wants you to."

"I don't think God will be upset at me for going away to school mom. Plus, I'm going to school for choirs. Why won't you be ok with that?"

"If you want to be fast and leave that's on you. Don't be mad when it doesn't work out for you when you do leave," she said as she walked out the kitchen.

She had upset me to the max. I don't see why leaving Atlanta was a big deal. I just wanted to make a way for myself. I want to be a singer, and I shouldn't have to stay here to do that. Finishing making my breakfast and tuning my mother out, I was upset at how she was acting. The fact that she said I wasn't nothing like my sister was a slap in the face. How can she say that I cant sing? She feels as if she and Leah are the only ones who can sing. It just wasn't fare. I know what I want to do and being saved wasn't going to stop that.

I left out the house right on time to walk to school; alone. Candi was in the house sick, and Justin still hadn't came by. I was begging to think that he was upset at me for not wanting to skip school with him. Him out of all people should know how important it was the last two years of school was. I also didn't want him getting the wrong impression. Even though I did like him, I just wanted him to respect how I felt.

As I walked down the path that I always go, the guy that had kissed me was standing at the corner again. This time he was standing their alone. Putting my head down I walked passed him.

"Hey mama. I just wanted to say that I was sorry for what I did to you," he said.

"Yeah, that was a really stupid thing you did. Trying to make yourself look goo in front of your friends was dumb," I replied. "Where are they anyway?"

"Well, I'm sorry. I had been looking for you, but you never walk this way anymore. Can I walk you to school?" he asked. "They locked up."

"What they do? Aren't you supposed to be in school too?"

"Na, I graduated a few years ago. I used to go to your school though. They robbed a store. A pretty girl like you don't have a boyfriend? Why are you always walking alone?"

"No. I'm not allowed to have a boyfriend."

"I bet that's boring. Too bad, I could have made a nice boyfriend for you."

"Oh really? How is that?"

"You have to let me show you, but since you can't have a boyfriend, I guess I can't huh?"

"I never said that you couldn't. I just said I wasn't allowed to have a boyfriend." As he was touching my hair I began to hum and sing to myself.

"Oh, you can sing huh?"

"Yeah."

"Do you have a phone. I can put my number in it and call you tonight. But you have to text me first though."

"Ok," I said. I gave him my phone out my purse and he put his number in it. I couldn't help but to smile from ear to ear. "I have bible study tonight. Do you go to church?"

"Na, I ain't never been. By the way my name is Duke. What's your name?"

"Armoni." He was looking real cute with his chocolate self. I wasn't sure why he was all in my face, but I was enjoying it. "How old are you?" I asked him as I stepped on their stairwell of my school.

"I'm 18, how old are you?"

"I just turned 16 this year. My birthday was a few months ago."

"Oh, ok cool. Well you go head in school. Call me tonight little mama."

"Ok, I will."

"Fa real, I want to talk to you tonight," he said.

I agreed with him and I headed into the school building. I was really feeling myself. The smile that I had on my face was not leaving. I didn't care what my mom said at this point, I was going to call him tonight too. I was 16, and he was 18. He didn't seem like a bad guy even though he stole a kiss, but I liked it too. Plus, he was way too cute to forget.

Going to my first class with my head up high, my hair hanging down my back, and my books in my hand. I was feeling like I was on top of the world. Hearing the snickering and laughter in class from my peers wasn't even bothering me anymore. It was like I was getting use to the jokes. The only thing they could talk about was me being in church. My grades were better than theirs, and I was passing all of my classes. My GPA was at a 3.5 and it was going up. I didn't really have to do much else to get into college.

After going to all of my classes and eating lunch, I was ready to go home. It was Friday, all my homework was already finished. I couldn't wait to get home to text Duke. At least he gave me his number. Justin didn't even bother to want to be in touch with me, so now he wasn't even my interest anymore. As soon as I got home I texted Duke to see what he was up to.

"Hey Duke, it's Armoni. What are you doing?"

"Oh, nothing boo. I was just thinking about your pretty a**. I didn't think you was gon' text me."

"Oh, really? I wasn't sure at first. Didn't think that you would text me back. What you doing?"

"Noting at the crib about to go hang out with some of my friends. You think you can sneak out?"

"I don't know. I have to go to church tonight with my parents."

"Dang, that sucks. I really wanted to see you. It's Friday, why you gotta' go to church?"

"Bible study."

"Can you skip that and come see me? I promise I wont keep you out late."

"I don't know. I just got home we leave in a few hours."

"Well text me back and let me know what she says."

"Ok. I will try."

"Ok cutie," he said.

I was super excited at this point. I had to find a way to see Duke. The fact that he texted me back was a plus, he didn't have to even speak to me. I don't know why I was super excited over this guy. He wasn't a Christian, nor did he go to church. My mother would kill me if she knew I was even taking to somebody like him. Justin for some reason was way too normal for me. He was just the person my mom wanted me to date; when it was time.

A couple hours had passed, and it was time for all of us to go to bible study. This was the first time in years I was going to lie to my parents and skip out on church. So, as they got ready for church I prepared myself. I laid in my bed with a hot rag over my head, and I also drank some milk. Since I'm lactose intolerant it made me use the bathroom. My parents had to let me stay home. Putting my plan into action I called for my mother.

"MOM!" I yelled from my room. "MOM PLEASE COME HERE!" I yelled again. Hearing her feet run up the stairs and swing open my bedroom door.

"What's wrong Armoni?" she asked in a frantic.

"Ugg, I don't feel good mom. My stomach hurts really bad, and I feel really hot," I told her. She placed her hand on my forehead, and touch my stomach.

"Oh, my Lord, you are burning up baby. What did you eat?"

"It had to be something from school," I lied. "I can't stop using the bathroom either."

"Well you cant go to bible study tonight. You need to get some rest. I'm going to bring you some water, and you stay right in this bed and sleep."

"Yes ma'am."

As she walked out the room I started to smile. My sister Candi and my brothers were going to church with my parents, and I was going to have the house all to myself. I felt a big tingling feeling take over my body. Was this what lying felt like? If so, if felt good. I finally was able to be a 16-year-old and stay home. My mom brought me some water and crackers, kissed me on my forehead and left. When I heard the door close creeped down the stairs to see if they were gone. The way our house was set up I was able to see the living room from the stairs. the coast was clear. I immediately texted Duke to see where we were meeting.

"Hey Duke, my parents are gone. Where did you want to meet at?" I texted him. I waited for about ten minutes to see if he would text me back, but he didn't. I called him instead. The phone rang a few times.

"Hello,' he said sounding like he was sleep.

"Hey Duke, it's me Armoni. I thought you wanted to meet up tonight?"

"Oh, my bad shorty. I'm chillin' with my boys. I totally forgot about it. Where you at?"

"I'm at home. My family all went to bible study. I acted like I was sick so I could see you," I told him.

"Oh, fa real? You told yo' folks you were sick. Shorty you wild. You really wanted to see me that bad?"

"Yeah. I mean I thought you wanted to see me too."

"You know I do. Give me a min. What time will your parents be back?"

"Um, they should be gone for the next couple of hours."

"Ok. Let me get rid of them. I will text you when I'm on my way. You live on Shelton St.?"

"Yeah. I live in the big brown house with the Nissan in the driveway."

"Ok. Here I come."

We hung up the phone and I got dressed. I went into Candise room and I took a pair of her jeans, a shirt, and a pair of her shoes out of her closet. I was not about to wear a skirt nor turtle neck to see him. I took my hair out of the pony tail that I had and brushed it down. I went down stairs to sit in the living room to wait. As I sat my mom called me. I got so nervous that I ignored her call. I was hoping that she figured that I was sleep and not call back, but she did. My phone started ringing again.

"Hello," I said in a soft voice.

"Are you ok baby?" she asked. "Are you feeling any better?"

"No ma'am. My stomach still hurts really bad. I just came down stairs to get me some more crackers," I lied.

"If you don't feel better by tomorrow I'm going to take you to the doctors," she added.

"Ok," I said. I just wanted to get her off the phone. "I think it was just something that I ate."

"Well get some rest. We should be home in a few hours. Hopefully your dad doesn't talk all night tonight."

I just laughed her off and we hung up. As I was still waiting on Duke to text me; I dozed off on couch. I was getting bored that I didn't even notice that I was getting sleepy. Not sure how long I was sleep, but my phone rang loud in my ear that I woke up. when I looked it had Dukes name on the screen. I rushed to answer it.

"Hello?"

"Yeah shorty. I'm sitting outside. You gone come out or what?"

"Yeah, here I come." Throwing on my jacket to cover up a little bit; I went out to meet him. he was sitting on our bottom step. "Hey there," I greeted him.

"What's good ma. Was you busy or sumthin'?"

"No, I dozed off waiting on you," I said smiling.

"Oh, my bad. My boys wasn't trying to leave. What time your parents coming back?"

"Like around ten. They at bible study. My dad is the pastor so, he can keep them for a while."

"Word? Well what you wanna do? We gone sit out here all night?"

"Um, what do you have in mind? I mean we can go in the house if you want, or we can sit in my car. I'm not allowed to drive it, but we can sit in it."

"Why can't you drive it. What you don't know how?"

"I don't have my license yet."

"Oh. So that means we cant take a ride? I promise I won't wreck it."

"Um….. I don't know Duke. I just got it. Can you drive?"

"Um, yeah. Come on lets go for a ride. I want to show you something."

I looked up at him and I got this funny feeling in my stomach. I didn't want to drive my car without my parents knowing, but he said he knew how to drive. What could it hurt? What could go wrong. Leaving him still sitting on the steps; I went into the house and grabbed my keys. When I came back out he was already standing by the driver door with his hand out.

"I'll drive. Come one I know a place we can go."

I just went along with him. I didn't ask any question, nor dispute him. we got into the car and drove off.

Apart of me knew that this was wrong, but what could it hurt? We were just taking a ride, and he was driving really great. Sitting their quiet he turned on the radio. The music he listened to was loud and had a lot of cursing in it. I have never listened to that kind of music before, so I didn't know how to react to it. I just held my head down as he drove.

That's when things took a turn for the worse. He got a phone call and he went through a red light. He began to speed and argue with who ever it was he was talking to. He started cursing and yelling, and I became terrified.

"You need to slow down Duke, Please take me home."

"I can't right now. I have to go check on my brother. He just got jumped. I will take you home later shorty," he said.

"No; Duke, take me home now. this is my car and your driving all wrong. What if you get pulled over."

"We won't. Just chill out. I will take you home after I check on my brother."

"Duke your scaring me. Take me home now. Better yet pull over. I'll take myself home."

He ignored me. He kept driving faster and faster going through every red light almost crashing into other cars. At this point I didn't know what to do. He was not listening to me at all. As I kept telling him to slow down he still was doing the opposite. We finally came to a fast stop where it was a bunch of kids fighting and yelling. After putting the car in park and he jumped out. It was nothing like I was used to; kids were fighting everywhere. I hid in the car scared. Things weren't getting any better. I opened up the passenger door and a girl ran up to me.

"You little whore! What are you doing with my man!" she yelled. She began to tug on my clothes.

"We are just friends. I didn't know he had a girlfriend." Now I was really terrified. I should have never let him talk me into leaving the house.

"Well now you do. You look like a softy," she added as she was grabbing on to me again.

"Get off of me. I just want to go home!" I yelled back.

"Your not going anywhere! You think you can just show up here with my man and not get dealt with?"

"I didn't know you was with him. He said he as single."

Before I knew it she was punching on me. I couldn't do anything but protect myself. I never had a fight before, and I had no clue what to do. I just started to swing back. Not being sure where my hands were landing, but I had to get her off of me. Next thing I knew I was running for my car door. Not sure how to drive home; I turned the keys and I drove off.

Panicking I drove home fast not noticing that I was speeding. When I turned the corner I almost crashed. I pulled over to catch my breath. Looking in the mirror I noticed that I had a cut above my eye and a busted lip. How was I going to explain this to my parents? I knew I should have went to church. Gathering my thoughts putting the car in drive; I sped home. I couldn't risk getting caught driving. When I looked at the clock it was almost 10:00. My parents were on their way home for sure. Parking the car in the driveway without a scratch. I went into the house with my heart beating a mile a minute.

Duke called my phone three times, but I didn't answer. He had gotten me in my first fight, now I had to explain my messed-up face to my parents. After laying there for a bit; my mom walked into my room. I hid my head as if I was sleep. I didn't want her to see my face at all. I was terrified. When she went into her room; I took my

shower and went to sleep. I didn't want to get into anything

else. Tomorrow was going to be very interesting. I just

hope they didn't notice anything.

Chapter 6: A Sinners Prayer

Last night was a complete disaster. I was not expecting it to go like that. The one time I wanted to have fun it goes left. I couldn't believe that Duke had gotten me into all that mess just that quick. I started to believe my mom when she said the devil was always around, and last night he showed up. God was the only reason I got home safe, I was upset with myself. When I woke up this morning I was still feeling sore. I didn't even feel like getting out of my bed. I heard my parents come in last night, and I didn't draw attention to myself going to talk to them. My face was still hurting, and I could barely open my right eye. Went into the bathroom to look in the mirror and my face was swollen. How was I going to explain this to my parents? What lie was I going to tell to get out of this one? I put a cold wash cloth on my face and sat on my bed. That's when Candi walked in.

"Girl what happened to you?" she asked being nosey. "What did you do?" she asked.

"Come in and shut the door. I have something to tell you. You have to promise me you wont tell mom nor dad?"

"I won't. Girl what happened? It look like you been in a fight or something," she said touching my face.

"Oww! That hurts." I moaned. My face was beyond sore. I had never felt nothing like this before.

"Armoni what happened?" she asked again.

"I got into a fight." The look on her face was crazy. Her eyebrows went up, then they went down.

"How? Who did you fight and when?"

"You know how I told mom that I was sick last night, and I couldn't go to bible study?"

"Yeah."

"Well, I wasn't really sick."

"Ok, but how did you get a black eye Armoni? What did you do?"

"Um……. This guy named Duke came over last night."

"You let a guy in the house?"

"No! Well kinda. We were sitting on the steps outside talking and……."

"What? That still don't explain the black eye though. What happened? Tell me or I am going to tell mom," Candi threatened me. I didn't want to tell her I took my car and let him drive. "Armoni stop playing with me! What happened?"

"I took my car last night Candi and some girl beat me up for being with duke. He wanted to drive my car so, I let him. Next thing I knew he's driving to a fight and he wouldn't bring me home," I blurted out.

"Armoni! Are you serious? Mama is going to kill you if you wrecked that car. How did you get home?"

"I fought the girl back and drove home. Candi I was really scared. Duke acted like I wasn't even there. I just left."

"Who is Duke? Armoni you are going to be in some serious trouble if mom and dad find out. Then you skipped out on church for a guy. I bet you don't even know him do you?"

"I kinda know him Candi. What am I going to do? I don't want mom to see me like this."

"You might as well come clean. It's the only way to stay right with God. You know that everything that you did was a sin, and mom won't be so happy about it. I know I've done some stuff, but I never skipped church."

"I can't tell her. She will make me read out the bible everyday for the rest of my life. You know how mom can get. She thinks everything is required to be punished with the bible."

"Well you better figure it out because here she come."

Climbing back into my bed covering up myself with my cover; I had no clue what to do next. My mom stopped Candi at my door and was talking to her. About what; I had no clue. I just hope that Candi didn't rat me out.

"Hey honey, how are you feeling?" she asked waling over to my bed.

"I feel a little better. My head just hurts. I hit my head when I was getting some tissue out the cabinet last night," I lied.

"Let me see, did you bruise it?"

"I don't know." I lifted my head from my pillow to show her my face.

"Oh, my Jesus, Armoni! Your face is purple. Did you put some ice on it?"

"No, ma'am. I had gotten light headed so I came back to lay down."

"Candi!" she yelled out for my sister. Candi came running back in my room.

"Yes ma'am?"

"Go to the kitchen and get me an ice-pack. Your sister has an black-eye." Candi left back out my room. Turning back around looking at my face, my mother started to look funny.

"What's wrong mom?" I asked.

"Your eye. It look like you have a fist mark. You hitting it on the cabinet wont have your face looking like this. What really happen?"

"I told you mom." Candi came back with the ice-pack and I placed it on my face. "It was an accident. I wasn't paying attention."

"It still doesn't sound right Armoni. Just tell me the truth. I promise I won't get mad."

When she said that I knew it was over. Either I told her the truth and she get mad and start praying, or I lie to her still and she still pray. I was stuck between a rock and a hard place. I didn't want to tell on myself, but for some odd reason the holy ghost wouldn't let me keep lying to her. I lifted my body off the bed to sit up. putting my head down and let out a big sigh.

"Well last night after you left for church I I I...."

"You what Armoni? Spit it out child. What did you do?" I looked up at my mom then looked up at Candi. She was looking at me crazy. "In the name of Jesus."

"Mom I hit her in the eye last night," Candi blurted out."

"You did what!" mom yelled. "What was you doing to hit her in the eye?"

"We were playing when we got back. It was an accident."

"Is that what happened?" she asked me.

"Yes ma'am."

"Father God." She placed her hands on my head and began to pray. "Lord God I am asking you to heal Armoni eye. I don't know what possessed them to be in here fighting in my house. Please place your hands on these two so that they understand that fighting is not the answer. Also shield their tongues from the lies that they have told. Lying is a sin Lord and I don't want you to condemn them for what they know not. You know their hearts Lord and you know their love. Please have mercy on their souls in the name of Jesus I pray. Amen."

She got off my bed and didn't say another word to me. Candi walked out behind her and didn't say anything either. I felt bad. I didn't ask my sister to lie for me, and now she might be in trouble too. My parents didn't like for us to fight, especially if it was physical. I felt like I got away with what I did, but then again I didn't. I know I wasn't going to live this down by Candi, nor God.

The longer I sat there the worse I felt. It was like now I couldn't stop telling lies. I had to keep up with what I was saying, but it was getting harder. The only thing that I knew that would fix it was prayer. I put my head down and I prayed for myself. I didn't wasn't to turn my back on God. Right in the middle of my prayer my phone rang. The first rule of prayer is to never break your prayer, but when I glanced at my phone it was Duke.

"Hello," I said with an attitude.

"Hey ma, are you good?" he asked.

"No, but I will be. Why are you calling me anyway. Don't you have a girlfriend to tend to?"

"No, she's not my girlfriend. She was upset because I didn't want to be with her anymore. I didn't even know she was there."

"Well she was, and she messed up my face. I had to lie to my mom about what happened."

"You didn't wreck the car did you?"

"No. No thanks to you I got home safe. My mama seen my eye this morning and she started praying for me."

"Ha, ha, ha. Prayed for you? Why?" he asked laughing.

"It's not funny. You almost got me into a lot of trouble. My sister lied and said she hit me in my eye."

"Did your mom believe her?"

"Yeah. I think she did. She says she did, but I can't tell. She walked out my room not saying a word."

"Well I want to see you if that's cool. I want to make sure you're ok."

"I don't know. I really don't feel right about this anymore. I feel like God is punishing me for going against him."

"Awe here you go with that Christian stuff again. You know that the bible not all real."

"Don't say that," I said getting upset.

"I mean it ain't. My mama ain't take us to church. She didn't believe it was important."

"So, your saying God isn't important?" I asked him.

"I mean I do, but I don't. He ain't did much for me or my family. If he was a true God; then why are their homeless people?"

"I don't know, but the God I serve is a good God," I added.

"I guess. Well ask God if I can see you then," he said mocking me.

"I have to go. My mom's calling me," I lied.

"Ahight. Just call me back later."

I was upset about what he said. How can one not believe in God, nor think the bible was real. I wasn't sure if I was going to talk to him anymore, but I really couldn't get mad at him. It wasn't his fault he don't know about God. I laid there thinking, and wondering. Even though I wanted to stay saved and make my parents happy, I still wanted to see what Duke was about. My mind was twisted. I went about the rest of my day in my room. I didn't know what else to do. I felt like the devil was twisting my arm. He was giving me temptation and I don't know how to handle it one bit.

Chapter 7: Saints Gossip

Today was going to be a long day. We had to go to church for a minister that was coming from another church. When we had to go to church for things like this; it was an all-day affair. First we was going out to eat for breakfast. Then we had to get the church ready, and after that we had to also feed that church. I just wanted to do what other normal 16-year old's did. After we all got dressed we were going to eat. I was excited about that too because we always went to Quincy's. It was like a big buffet kind of place. I loved living in Atlanta. It was a lot of different food places here.

After talking to Duke, a couple of weeks ago after my fight; I really didn't say much else to him. Justin was still trying his hardest to get my attention at church, but I just ignored him. It was no excuse why he stood me up that day, and I still didn't want to be bothered by him. I had been doing really good not going against my Christian

lifestyle, but it was so hard not to. After telling so many lies

to my mom I started to feel really bad. Then being ok with

my sister lying for me wasn't sitting well with me. Apart of

me felt as if my mom knew I was lying, but how was I

supposed to tell her. She already has doubts about me

leaving for college, and what I have done confirms what

she was saying.

It was about 9:00 in the morning and I had already

had my dress out for today. It was 85 degrees outside, and I

still had to put my stockings on. No matter what kind of

skirt or dress I wore, I had to put stockings on under it. My

mom would have a cow had I not. Candise had on a skirt

and a really tight shirt that made her chest stick out. I know

that if my mom saw it she was going to spaz. I guess that's

why Candi put on a jacket to cover it up.

I was surprised when I saw Leah walk pass by my

room. She hadn't came home from school in a while. She

must have gotten tired of campus. My twin brothers were going too. I was happy about it too because Drew was bringing his son Maliki with him. I couldn't wait to see him either. He was almost one, and his mom barely let us see him. I know when we go to church the elders in the church are going to talk about him. That's what they did. When the younger generation did something that goes against their beliefs; they gossip about it.

When it was time for us to leave we all had to ride in the car with my parents. I wasn't sure how we all were going to fit because we all were not so little anymore. Then since we had Drew's baby with us we were all squished. Standing outside waiting for my parents to come out I noticed that Duke had rode passed. He was in the passenger seat with some girl driving. Now I'm not one to jump to conclusion, but it didn't sit well with me. I took my phone out to text him.

"Um… So, your just going to ride past me with some other girl?" I said with an angry face emoji. I wasn't sure why I was so mad about it, but he was just trying to see me. "I knew you were a lire. You just gone ride past my house like that with that girl?" I added.

"Man look you made it clear the other day that you wasn't messing with me. What do you care church girl. Ain't like you was gone give it up to me anyway." I looked at my phone in disgust.

"That's all you wanted to talk to me for?"

"What else did you think it was lil mama? You really thought I was going to be a church nigga? HA HA HA HA ! Yeah that will never happen."

I put my phone in my pocket. I had an attitude. Still waiting for my parents to come out, everybody else came out to wait on them too. It was way too hot to be standing out here. I wasn't sure what was going on, but my dad came storming outside.

"Is everyone ready to go?" he yelled.

"We been ready for over an hour," I mumbled under my breath."

"What was that?" he asked turning around looking at us. Trying to find out which one of us was talking back. "Get in the car, we are already late as it is." We all tried to get in my dad Ford Fusion, but it wasn't enough room.

"This is not going to work mom," I said. "Drew why can't we get into your car?"

"Because something wrong with it. I need to get it fixed. Why we cant ride in Leah car?" Drew asked.

"Because I need my gas for school," she complained. "Mom can I drive Armoni car?" she asked.

"That's up to Armoni. Since she never took her drivers test it's going to just sit here." I was not liking the fact she asked to drive my car. "It's way more room in there, we can just follow behind yawl," she suggested.

"Ion want nobody driving my car but me. Besides none of yawl want to give me driving lessons, so why should I let yawl drive it?"

"Man stop being on that before I tell mama your secret," Drew said. Everybody started to look at me funny. I didn't know what he was talking about, but I didn't want to get in trouble either.

"What secret?" my mom asked. "What did you do Armoni?"

"I don't have a secret. Mom can I drive it if Leah is with me?"

"Yes, but we have to leave now. We are already late so, what ever yawl are going to do we need to hurry up," my mother added.

"You better drive careful too Armoni. No speeding and put on your seat belt," my dad said.

Drew, his son, Leah and I got out my dads car and went to my car. I was still kind of nervous from the last time I was behind the wheel. I wasn't sure how I was able to get home without a scratch, but I did. Getting into the driver seat and they got into the back. Leah wasn't making things any better by talking mess to me.

"Candise told us about your joy ride the other day," she stated.

"What you mean? I didn't do anything," I said back.

"So, you didn't take your car with some dude? You need to let me get my hands on him for letting you get a

black-eye. That's a b**** move he did man. What you
doing talking to some hood nigga anyway?" Drew said.

"Candi runs her mouth too much. I just wanted to
go for a ride. I didn't know I was going to get into a fight.
He called me and said he was sorry."

"I don't care about his sorry sis." As he was talking
I started the car. "Put your seat belt on and put your foot on
the break before you put it in drive," Drew explained to me.

"Yeah, the last time we talked you was asking me
about sneaking out or wanting to say home. If you have to
go through all this trouble to talk to this guy, you don't
need to talk to him, little sis," Leah said.

"But I really like him, or at least I think I do. I don't
know anymore. I just know that mom and dad won't go for
it. Being in the church is frustrating sometimes. It's too
many rules."

"Yeah well that's why I just go with the flow. You see I just go only to please mama. My son about to be one and I don't care how nobody feels. I'm grown."

I pulled off right behind dad as Leah and Drew were still talking to me. I really wasn't trying to hear what they had to say either because I felt like they were attacking me. Trying to pay attention to the rode, my phone began to ring.

"You better not answer that," Leah said.

"I wasn't. can you see who it is for me please?" I asked her. She looked through my purse and pulled out my phone.

"It's Duke."

"Man, why is he still calling you? You want me to say something to him?"

"No. It's ok. I just won't answer or call him back," I said being unsure.

I had drove all the way to the restaurant without any issues. I was glad too. They was getting on my last nerve. I just wish they would just stay out my business. It wasn't like I was having sex with him or anything. We were just friends, and I was happy about that. We all got out the car and met up with mom and dad. They were already in line for us to get a table. As soon as I turned around to say something to Candi about her ratting me out; Justin and his family walked in the door. I put my head down and kept walking.

"Look Justin isn't that your girlfriend," his little brother said.

"Shut up before mom and dad hears you. And no, she isn't my girlfriend."

"Yawl stop all that playing," his mom said breaking them up.

We got to our table and they sat at the table next to us. Every time we see someone from church we always had to sit near them. It never failed. My dad being a pastor had all the church members flocking to us if they seen him. I didn't want to even be in the same area as Justin. He stared at me like I was a fish in a tank. He didn't speak, nor wake he just kept staring. I didn't say anything to him either. I heard the rumors about him and one of the other girls from church. He must know that I know. We were at the restaurant for about an hour before it was time for us to leave. We had to do more family stuff before church.

Getting back into my car this time it was Leah, Candi, Duke and me. My parents ended up taking the baby with them. My mom wanted to spend as much time with him as she could. my dad wanted us to go to a homeless shelter and help pass out lunches, but none of us wanted to go. It was like we had to spend all of our time doing things that he wanted us to do. We always had to paint an image that we were this perfect family. We were far from a

perfect family. We followed behind him as he drove all

around town. I was getting bored, so I turned down a

different street.

"Where are you going Armoni?" Candi asked.

"I was going to the mall. I know yawl don't want to

go to the shelter today."

"Dad is going to kill us if we don't show up," Leah

whined.

"So, what. I'm just about tired of dad and his rules.

We always have to play it safe because he's the pastor.

Don't you get tired of being bored?"

"Yeah, but…"

"Armoni, Just drive. They wont miss us anyway.

I'm pretty sure that they have enough help," Drew said.

"Plus, I can get some clothes for my son."

"I guess," Candi replied. "You must not want to be around Justin. Yeah I heard about yawl kissing in his dads office at church," she added.

"Shut up Candi! You don't know what your talking about. I never kissed him." I lied. How in the world did she know what happened?"

"Yeah well, Shelly told me that Justin told his brother that yawl did. And he she said that he took you out to eat too, and he kissed you again and you ran off crying."

"I didn't run off crying. I ran into the building because the bell rang. Shelly doesn't know what she's talking about."

"So, you did kiss him," Drew said.

"No bro I didn't. He kissed me. There is a big difference."

"Dang Armoni, you getting kissed by everybody. I leave for a few weeks and your cutting up. If mama found out she's going to make you read from that bible for sure."

"Shut up Leah." Right as we were about to pull into the mall parking lot my mom called my phone. I didn't want to answer, nor did I want to hear her mouth. "Answer it Leah."

"No! You're the one who wanted to come to the mall. You answer it."

"Huh, You suck," I said snatching my phone out of her hand. "Hello," I answered.

"Umm where are you? Did you get lost?" she asked.

"No mom we didn't get lost. Drew needed to get some things for the baby, so we came to the store."

"Don't you think that could have waited until tomorrow or something?"

"No ma'am he needs diapers, milk, and some clothes. So, we are getting that then heading to the church."

"Ok, well hurry up. Your father is upset, and he said you better make sure you put the gas back in the tank."

"Yes ma'am."

We was home free. They all started yelling and screaming in my ear because I was able to get our mom to let us stay at the mall. Now all we had to was get some of the things I said, and we were good. We stayed at the mall the whole time. I saw some clothes that I wanted, and shoes. We went into about six stores. That's when I saw Duke and that girl again. She was the same one that punched me in the face. I didn't say a word, only because I knew it would have been all bad. Leah and Drew would have got in a lot of trouble over me. So, I just ignored them.

After Drew got that he needed; we got some pretzels then we headed to the church. Drew showed my mom what he got, and she didn't even get mad at him, but the look she gave me. I knew then I was in big trouble.

As she greeted everyone that was coming in, she told me to go sit down in the first pew. I knew then I was in deep crap. Wasn't sure exactly why she was so upset, but we were at church so, she didn't show it. Leah and Candi went to the choir stand to sing as the other visiting church came in. My dad was siting in his seat and my brothers were sitting by the musicians. They both played, so that's where they had to sit.

I felt embarrassed that I wasn't able to sing with my sisters. I sat all the way at the end and held my head down. I didn't even want to be there anymore. As I sat there watching everyone else enjoy their time two ladies behind me was getting on my nerves.

"Girl did you hear what happened to sister Allice daughter?" one of them asked the other.

"Nawl girl what happened?" the other woman replied. As they were trying to whisper I heard everything.

"Well, I heard from my husband that she was cheating on her husband with somebody from her job. And she has a nerve to be up there singing for the Lord."

"Girl you have to be lying."

"Girl I'm not. She was caught cheating. They was saying that her daughter they have together wasn't his."

"Mmmn, that's a whole lot of sinning. She needs to be asking God for forgiveness and be sat down. How she up there singing for the Lord and she ain't being faithful to her husband?"

"He sure is fine ain't he. Look at him over there playing the drums."

"Shut up girl. Your something else."

I didn't know what to do either laugh at how thirsty they sound, or to be mad at what they were saying. Who else were they talking about behind their backs. I just got up and went to the bathroom. Even though I knew my mom would get mad, but I just couldn't sit and listen to them so called church women talk about someone else. As soon as I went into the bathroom the gossiping got worse. The two girls that always talking about Justin were sitting in the lounge talking. As I walked passed I could feel the mess coming. Once I closed the door to my stall it started. First came the laughing, then they started whispering, then it got louder.

"I don't know why she think that Justin wants her. He said that her house was dirty, and she was broke," one of them said. I knew it was a lie because our house was spotless. And I always had money. I just laughed. "She has some nerve thinking that she better than me. She so ugly."

"Her sister Leah goes to school with my sister and she said that she heard Leah wasn't a virgin. Said that she been dating some guy there,"

"That family is so nasty. My mama said the pastor was sleeping around."

"Well, I haven't told anybody, but he was trying to put his hands in my dress last Sunday," she stated.

"Why you didn't tell your mom. That's nasty. I wish he would try and touch me." I busted out the bathroom stall enraged.

"You shouldn't tell lies about people like that. Especially my dad. He's not no way interested in you. You're only 18, and he's married with a family. Keep lying on my dad and watch what I do to your face," I replied back.

"Get your ugly a** out my face."

"Make me." As I stood there in her face ready to punch the lights out of her my sister walked in.

"Armoni what is going on?" she asked pulling me away from the girls face.

"This idiot said dad was touching her and I know she's lying. Dad wouldn't do anything like that."

"Yeah our dad isn't like that so, I would suggest for you to take it back," Candi said in the girl face.

"Whatever," she said walking away.

I wasn't really sure if she was telling the truth, but Candi and I just walked back in the sanctuary as if nothing had happened. I wouldn't dare to agree that my dad would do something like that, nor tell my mom what was said. The fact that I knew she was upset at me for some reason could be why she said what she said, but out of all things to say; she said my dad molested her. I was pissed for the rest of the night. I had so many questions in my head that only god would be able to answer. I just payed to him hoping

that what I was told wasn't true.

Chapter 8: Sinners Are Saints

After that retard of a girl said that my dad touched her, I began to think on it hard. I wasn't saying that he did, but maybe it was someone else in the church who did. Some of the ministers in the church can be a bit too friendly. I had me think about the time we were in revival and one of the visiting ministers was a bit too close to me. His hands seems as if they were wondering, and the kisses on the cheeks were way too close to my face.

I didn't think much of it because I was young, so I just let it go. It was mid-April and I was ready to move on to the twelfth grade. I was still passing all of my classes, but it was like my whole year was wasted. I guess because I didn't do any of the fun activities that they had. I didn't go to any of the games, I didn't go to any of the dances, nor did I participate in the parties. Prom was coming up and I just knew that my parents weren't going to let me go, so I didn't even bother to ask. I had finally got my licenses after begging Leah to take me driving, so I was able to leave without asking someone to take me places. I was happy about that too because I get bored and I just want to leave.

I still didn't say much to Duke even though he continued to call and text me. I just gave him short answers. I was still upset at him for putting me in that situation, but a part of me wanted to see him. I figured I'd give myself some time. having to ware make-up to cover up my black eye was no fun. I didn't want him to get me into anymore trouble. It was something about him though that just had my nose wide open.

After a couple of weeks had passed. A strange letter had came in the mail from some woman. It was addressed to my dad. I wanted to know what it said so bad that I opened it. The letter read.

Dear Pastor,

I know that I shouldn't be writing you, but I just couldn't help myself. After our first date I couldn't get you out of my mind.

Reading the first few sentences gave me a sick feeling in my stomach. Who was this woman, and what was she doing seeing my dad? I took the letter up to my room and I continued to read it.

I know that you're married, but I just can't let you go. You told me that you were going to leave your wife and I believed you. I am not sure what's going on but me and your son needs you. He hasn't seen you since he was two and now he's five. I hope that this letter reaches you and not your wife. I really don't want her to find out like this. I hope to hear from you real soon. My number has not changed.

Love, Joanne

When I finished reading the letter I just began to cry. Maybe this was the reason why my parents fought so much. My dad was having an affair and my mom found out. I just couldn't believe it. He was so big on being a perfect Christian, he was being the biggest sinner. He has all these people looking up to him to lead him in a direction of salvation, and he's the doing the sinning. I just couldn't believe what I was seeing. I wasn't sure if I was to give it to my mom or throw it away. After a few minutes I decided to place it in my sock drawer. Maybe it was a good explanation behind it.

Today was Wednesday and we had to go to church, but I had other plans. At one of our revivals that my dad had I met this super choir. They were so amazing that I wanted to join them. The only problem was that the choir was held in NCU. I wanted to go to school, but I had never thought about North Carolina. My mom was totally against it. I just wanted to follow my dreams of becoming a gospel singer. Today was their pre-entry tryouts and I was

definitely going. After my last class I didn't even go

straight home. I went to Mount Saint Bonville Church in

Rockdale. Now I don't normally go to this side of Georgia,

but I had to so I could ensure a spot.

When I arrived the nine was already long. I felt like

I was waiting in line for a concert or to get into a nightclub.

Going behind my parents backs wasn't what I planned on

doing, but I knew that that wasn't going to let me. I just

told my mom that I had some after school work to do. I

couldn't pass up this opportunity. It was now or never. I

didn't want to be stuck here like Leah. She still hasn't left

Atlanta yet.

I stood in the line for about an hour before I even

reached the inside of the church. It was so many people

waiting to be seen. Knowing that this was something that I

wanted for myself I couldn't let none of them out sing me.

Listening to them all sing one by one; my nerves got the

best of me. My hands began to sweat, and my throat started to get dry. Right when I was about to turn around and walk out; I heard a familiar voice.

"My dad is a minister in Atlanta," he said. "I'm just trying to make something of myself."

It was Justin. I had never in my life heard him sing before. I wasn't even sure if he knew how. With him being here gave me more reasons to be nervous. Every time I sang in front of him he'd give me the chills. When I lifted my head up to see where he went he noticed me. I instantly put my head back down. That's when I felt a tap on my shoulder.

"Yes," I said still holding my head down.

"I was wondering when you were going to show up," he said.

"Why? How did you even know I was going to be here?" I asked him. He grabbed my face and lifted up my head.

"Because you have a beautiful voice. If anybody should get into this choir; it should be you." I was flattered. Even though he had been ignoring me. He still knew how to make me smile.

"What are you doing here? I didn't know you knew how to sing."

"Yeah? Well I don't think anybody did; not even my parents. I just wanted to see if I had a shot."

"It doesn't hurt to try."

"Yeah; your right."

Instead of him going back in his spot; he stayed with me. As the line move I noticed that he was standing really close to me. He smelled so good in his black suit, his fine hair, white teeth, and his light skin. I couldn't help but to stare at him. He was fine and he knew it as well as other girls. we got closer and closer until we were up next. He let me go before him.

"Name?" the young woman asked me.

"Armoni Carmichael," I replied.

"Age and grade?"

"16, and I'm a junior in high school."

"What will you be singing?"

"Umm. The Battle is not yours by Yolonda Adams," I said with a nervous voice.

"Ok. Take it away when your ready." With everyone staring at me I closed my eyes and began to sing.

"There is no pain Jesus can't feel. No hurt He cannot heal. All things work according to His perfect will. No matter what you're going through. Remember God is using You. For the battle is not yours, it's the Lord's.

There's no sadness Jesus can't feel, And there is no sorrow
that He cannot heal. For all things work according to the
Master's holy Will, No matter what you're going through,
Remember that God is only using You. For the battle is not
yours, it's the Lord's, It's the Lord's, yes, it's the Lord's,
Hold your head up high don't you fright, It's the Lord's, it's
the Lord's. Yes, it's the Lord's. The next thing I heard was
clapping and yelling.

"Wow, you were amazing. What I want you to do id
go talk to the choir director Shannon. She will give you all
the paper work you need. Welcome to NCU's Gospel
Choir," she said shaking my hand.

I couldn't believe it. I finally was able to show what
I had. I was finally able to step out of the shadow if my
singing family and make a mark of my own. I went to talk
to the choir director, and she had me fill out some forms
that would get me on campus before I even started college.
They were also having me fill out a form to see if I would

qualify for a scholarship. I was praying that I did because I didn't want to have to ask my parents for anything. I walked out of that church thanking God. I praised him like I ain't never prayed before. As I walked to my car Justin walked out.

"Armoni!" he yelled for me. I turned around with a smile on my face to see what he wanted.

"Did you get through too?" I asked him.

"Yeah, so I guess I'll be seeing you at NCU."

"I guess so. I'm so excited right now. This is something that I have always wanted. I didn't want to have to stay here for school."

"Won't your parents be upset? I know mine will be. I didn't even tell them I was coming," he said.

"I didn't either. You know my father ain't going for it. He already had my sister Leah stay behind," I replied.

"Wow, well I hope you get in then so that we can be near each other."

"Yeah that would be nice. I would have someone to talk to. I'm kind of scared though," I mentioned.

"You don't have to be; I will take care of you. Where are you headed now?"

"On my way home now. Where are you about to go?" I asked.

"I was going to get something to eat. Did you want to go with me?" Jason asked me.

"Sure. I haven't eaten since lunch. I will follow you in my car," I said.

"Ok."

I was excited that everything was looking up for me. And now that Justin was also going made it even better. He was slowly growing on me; even though that he has a lot of girls that wanted him too. For some reason I just couldn't not talk to him. After falling him for about ten minutes, he stopped at this little diner. I was starving too. When we stopped he came to my window.

"What's up? Is everything ok?"

"Yeah, I'm going to go in and get our food. We going to eat in your car; is that cool?"

"Yeah, that's fine."

I still couldn't stop smiling. It was like God was making everything fall in place. The more I tried to push Justin away; God placed him right back. As I waited for him to come back my dad called me. I didn't answer though. I didn't want him to tell me to come home. I was 16 and I really wanted to have some fun. I know I was going against the "Christian Rules" but I'm human. Justin came back out of the diner with food in his hands. I unlocked my door and let him in.

"That was fast," I said to him.

"Yeah, I just got us some hamburgers and fries. Is that cool with you?"

"Yeah," I replied.

"What's wrong?" he asked noticing my face.

"My dad just called me, but I didn't answer," I told him.

"Why not?"

"Because I didn't want him to know what I was doing. All he would have said was *"That's a sin to be with a guy and your not married. It's a sin to be alone with a guy without your parents.* I get irritated with that all the time."

"Yeah I feel you. My parents are the same way. God knows our hearts. What's wrong with eating burgers?"

"Right." I looked at him while he ate. I just couldn't believe he was sitting next to me. "So, are you talking to any of the girls from church?"

"Yeah."

"Oh, ok. Which one? Is it Shelly?" I asked being nosey.

"No, she's a singer and she's very pretty."

I looked at him clueless. I wasn't sure who he was talking about until he kissed me. He held my face close to his and continued to kiss me. I didn't even stop him either. Next thing I knew his hand was on my thigh then it was going up my skirt. I pushed his hand back.

"Wait, what are you doing?" I asked him nervously.

"Just lay back and relax," he replied.

I just laid back and closed my eyes. He did things to me that I was told was not ok to do until I was married. I was scared nervous and worried. It lasted for about an

thirty minutes. Once he finished he gave me a hug and told

me that he was going to come see me after school

tomorrow. I didn't know how to feel at this point. I drove

home with a lot on my mind. My parents were already

home and I knew it was time for me to hear their mouth. As

I went in I just went up to my room and shut the door. I

could still hear them yelling. It didn't bother me none. I just

took my shower, prayed, and went to bed.

Chapter 9: Three Years Later "Repent"

Now that I was out of school and in college, I was glad to be on my own. I decided that I was only going back home for the holidays. I attend NCU in North Carolina and I was enjoying myself. The day that I left I got a lot of flack from my parents, but I really didn't care.

After my junior year in high school I started doing whatever I wanted to do. Justin and I had started dating each other and I ended up getting pregnant. My parents were devastated, and they wanted me to get an abortion so that the church wouldn't find out. But Justin and I wanted to keep it, so we did. We both are here together in North Carolina with our beautiful daughter Alicia. She is going on three years old. I tried my best to make my parents happy, but I had to live for me too.

Being a Christian doesn't always mean that we have to be perfect. I have given my life to Jesus Christ, but I also make sure that I am happy. My daughter has two loving parents that take great care of her. Being in the choir for school and getting that scholarship paved my way for me. Justin on the other hand didn't get the scholarship. As much as his parents were mad that he left and got me pregnant; they still helped him. He also didn't join the choir, he just focused on his studies of being a doctor.

Every day I go to school and work to make a life for Alicia. It's very hard juggling being a working mom and being in school. My parents send her gifts, but they want nothing to do with me. I found out that the rumors about my dad was true, and it made me sick to my stomach. He cheated on my mom and had a whole other family with another woman. My mom didn't want to tell me, but I guess she felt ashamed. Everything that my dad taught me I questioned, but now that I was older; I really didn't care anymore how he felt.

Justin changed a lot too. He was not as into me as he was when we were in high school. I think after having Alicia he thought that things would be the same, but it wasn't. We barley have any time alone. He's either in class or out with his college friends. When he does come home he is playing with Alicia. I asked him if we were ever going to get married so that we wouldn't be living in sin; and he stated, since we started in sin we might as well stay in sin. I wasn't sure where we stood anymore.

Every Sunday we went to church down the street from where we stayed at. Since we wasn't married; we couldn't attend an apostolic church. The way that we lived was against their rules. We were what they called black-sliders. If we were at home I would have had been rebaptized, sat down, and ridiculed for the path that I went down. At times I wish I had listened to my mother, but then I realized that I was just human.

As I continued with my everyday life I knew that I had to make a choice. My chances of being a professional gospel singer was slim. I didn't even have enough time to even go to the school studio to record. It was like my life was going down-hill. Often times I cried and prayed to God and asked him if he was punishing me, but then I just say thank you. My life could have been worse off than what it was.

Being 19, a college student and a mom; I just figured that all I needed to do was as for forgiveness, so I did. For the first time in a long time I got down on my knees and prayed. Had I just did what I was supposed to do then maybe I wouldn't feel the way I did. Was my parents right this whole time? Or was I just being hard on myself?

Dear God,

I am coming to you today to ask you for forgiveness. I know that I was not doing anything that you wanted me to, but I tried. I'm still trying to live right, and make sure

that my daughter follows your every word. I am asking you

to forgive me for all my sins, and for falling short. As I

continue my journey I promise to keep you first. I can't

promise to be perfect and to do everything by the book, but

I will try. I just want to be a good mother to Alicia and give

her a great life. I know that since I'm not married that

things will be hard for me, but I know that I learned from

my mistake. Being a Christian really has it's test and I just

want to pass. Lord please forgive me for all of my sins. In

the name of Jesus, I pray…… Amen.

I said the same prayer everyday just asking god to

keep me and my family in his grace, I wanted to make sure

that I stayed rooted in my faith as much as possible. I didn't

want the worldly life to take full control over me, but that

was the way it was looking. Even though Justin an I were

together. I could feel the distance between us. As long as he

stayed constant in is daughters life I was happy. From here

on out it was all about her. I'm a Christian, and I walk by faith not sight. I sin because I'm human, and I will always ask God for forgiveness. Do you have your vessel in order?

THE END

Other Books By Kandy Kaine:

1)	When Revenge Takes Over part 1

2)	When Revenge Takes Over Part 2

3)	Becky With The Good Hair. (Victoria Secrets)

4)	A Killer Valentine

5)	Secrets Of An Unfaithful Lover Part 1

6)	Secrets Of An Unfaithful Lover Part 2

7)	Unbreakable Bonds

8) The Woman On Top

9) A Sinners Redemption "Searching For My Soul"

Here's How To Contact Me:

•	Email: lovinggod600@gmail.com

•	Instagram: kandy_kaine88

•	Twitter: kandykaine@kainekandy

Made in the USA
Columbia, SC
23 June 2022

62154842R00088